little Miss Fun

by Roger Hargreaves

D1395830

Little Miss Fun is as happy
as a lark.

Except when she is organising a party.

And then...

She is even happier than a lark.

Little Miss Fun simply adores parties.

And she likes to invite lots and lots
of people to her parties.

The other Sunday, there were a lot of people
making their way to Little Miss Fun's house.

Mr Funny was making funny faces.
Mr Lazy was yawning.
Mr Clumsy was falling over.

And Mr Tall was walking in very small steps . . .
so he would not arrive too early!

Mr Forgetful was not with them.
He was at home. Reading a book.
He'd forgotten all about Little Miss Fun's party!

"Never mind,"
laughed Little Miss Fun.
"We can start the party without him!"

She put a record on the record-player.

The record went round and round,
and the music played.

Little Miss Fun asked
Mr Clumsy to dance with her.

And he accepted.

Unfortunately, he stood on her right foot.

"Never mind," she laughed.

Then she ran off to ask Mr Lazy to dance.

Unfortunately, when he put his head on her shoulder, he fell asleep.

And almost flattened her!

"Never mind!" she laughed.

In less than an hour,
Little Miss Fun had made everybody dance:

...the Rumba and the Samba,

...the Rock-and-Roll and the Twist,

...the Charleston and the Cha-Cha-Cha.

Then she led everybody out into the garden.

And they danced all around the house.

All the flowers in the garden were trampled.

"Never mind!"
said Little Miss Fun.
"Let's go back indoors."

"Let's play Simon Says..."
she cried.

"Simon Says...put your feet in the air!"

There was a loud CRASH!

As Mr Tall's foot smashed through the window pane and shattered it!

"Never mind,"
laughed Little Miss Fun.

And she jumped onto the table
so she could pretend to be a clown
and make her friends laugh.

But nobody laughed.

No wonder!

Everybody was exhausted.

They had all fallen asleep.

"Never mind!" laughed
Little Miss Fun.

And she carried on pretending to be a clown.

Who was she doing it for,
now that everybody was asleep?

Well, she was doing it for a little bird
who had flown in through the broken window.

But there's someone else she is doing it for,
isn't there?

Why, for you, of course!

because you aren't asleep yet...

...but you will be soon.

3 Great Offers for MR. MEN Fans!

MR. MEN TOKEN

1 New Mr. Men or Little Miss Library Bus Presentation Cases

A brand new stronger, roomier school bus library box, with sturdy carrying handle and stay-closed fasteners.

The full colour, wipe-clean boxes make a great home for your full collection.

They're just £5.99 inc P&P and free bookmark!

☐ MR. MEN   ☐ LITTLE MISS (please tick and order overleaf)

2 Door Hangers and Posters

In every Mr. Men and Little Miss book like this one, you will find a special token. Collect 6 tokens and we will send you a brilliant Mr. Men or Little Miss poster and a Mr. Men or Little Miss double sided full colour bedroom door hanger of your choice. Simply tick your choice in the list and tape a 50p coin for your two items to this page.

PLEASE STICK YOUR 50P COIN HERE

Door Hangers (please tick)
☐ Mr. Nosey & Mr. Muddle
☐ Mr. Slow & Mr. Busy
☐ Mr. Messy & Mr. Quiet
☐ Mr. Perfect & Mr. Forgetful
☐ Little Miss Fun & Little Miss Late
☐ Little Miss Helpful & Little Miss Tidy
☐ Little Miss Busy & Little Miss Brainy
☐ Little Miss Star & Little Miss Fun

Posters (please tick)
☐ MR. MEN
☐ LITTLE MISS

3 Sixteen Beautiful Fridge Magnets – any 2 for £2.00! inc.P&P

They're very special collector's items!
Simply tick your first and second* choices from the list below
of any 2 characters!

1st Choice

- ☐ Mr. Happy
- ☐ Mr. Lazy
- ☐ Mr. Topsy-Turvy
- ☐ Mr. Bounce
- ☐ Mr. Bump
- ☐ Mr. Small
- ☐ Mr. Snow
- ☐ Mr. Wrong

- ☐ Mr. Daydream
- ☐ Mr. Tickle
- ☐ Mr. Greedy
- ☐ Mr. Funny
- ☐ Little Miss Giggles
- ☐ Little Miss Splendid
- ☐ Little Miss Naughty
- ☐ Little Miss Sunshine

2nd Choice

- ☐ Mr. Happy
- ☐ Mr. Lazy
- ☐ Mr. Topsy-Turvy
- ☐ Mr. Bounce
- ☐ Mr. Bump
- ☐ Mr. Small
- ☐ Mr. Snow
- ☐ Mr. Wrong

- ☐ Mr. Daydream
- ☐ Mr. Tickle
- ☐ Mr. Greedy
- ☐ Mr. Funny
- ☐ Little Miss Giggles
- ☐ Little Miss Splendid
- ☐ Little Miss Naughty
- ☐ Little Miss Sunshine

*Only in case your first choice is out of stock.

--- TO BE COMPLETED BY AN ADULT ---

To apply for any of these great offers, ask an adult to complete the coupon below and send it with the appropriate payment and tokens, if needed, to MR. MEN OFFERS, PO BOX 7, MANCHESTER M19 2HD

☐ Please send ____ Mr. Men Library case(s) and/or ____ Little Miss Library case(s) at £5.99 each inc P&P

☐ Please send a poster and door hanger as selected overleaf. I enclose six tokens plus a 50p coin for P&P

☐ Please send me ____ pair(s) of Mr. Men/Little Miss fridge magnets, as selected above at £2.00 inc P&P

Fan's Name _____

Address _____

_____ **Postcode** _____

Date of Birth _____

Name of Parent/Guardian _____

Total amount enclosed £ _____

☐ **I enclose a cheque/postal order payable to Egmont Books Limited**

☐ **Please charge my MasterCard/Visa/Amex/Switch or Delta account** (delete as appropriate)

Card Number

Expiry date ___/___   **Signature** _____

MR.MEN   LITTLE MISS
Mr. Men and Little Miss™ & ©Mrs. Roger Hargreaves